Miss Renée's Mice

By Elizabeth Stokes Hoffman
Illustrated by Dawn Peterson

Down East Books
Rockport, Maine

*For Renée Bowen, extraordinary
miniature maker, delightful friend,
and fellow Tiny Tim zealot.*

Miss Renée lived in a big house by the ocean.

The big house was full of little houses.

The little houses were full of little furniture and other beautiful things.

Miss Renée made the furniture herself out of maple and pine from the Maine woods. She made curtains and pillows and bedspreads out of the best calico she could buy.

She made a lot of other things, too: colorful rugs, and cups and plates and teapots, and electric lamps that really worked.

Miss Renée filled the bookcases with miniature books that she printed on a miniature printing press. She decorated each room with thimble-sized vases of pink and red and yellow tulips that she made from dainty bits of colored paper.

Practically anything a little house needed to be perfect, Miss Renée knew how to make.

When she was all done with a new house and feeling quite
pleased with herself, she bought plastic dolls and sat them
in the chairs.

The dolls were dull and didn't do anything, but she
thought the houses looked empty without them.

One night there was a terrible storm with ice and snow and sleet and wind.

BOOM! It blew down Miss Renée's barn.

The barn had been full of mice—but not anymore!

The mice moved into the big house.

Then they moved into the little houses.

The mice pitched the dolls out the windows and sat on the chairs. They slept in the beds. They switched the lights on and off. They pulled the books down from the shelves and read them.

They helped themselves to food from Miss Renée's pantry. They even found the secret drawer where she kept her chocolate.

The mice dressed up in the dolls' clothes and had wild parties.

What a mess! What noise! It was unbelievable.

Miss Renée's striped cat was too lazy to chase the mice away.

Miss Renée fretted about what to do. Night after night she lay awake, drumming her fingers on the pillow.

. . . Until she thought of a plan.

She sawed and whittled and hammered and nailed, and then she sanded and painted and varnished.

She stitched and sewed and sewed and stitched on her midget sewing machine, whistling an old sea chanty while she worked.

Finally she was done.

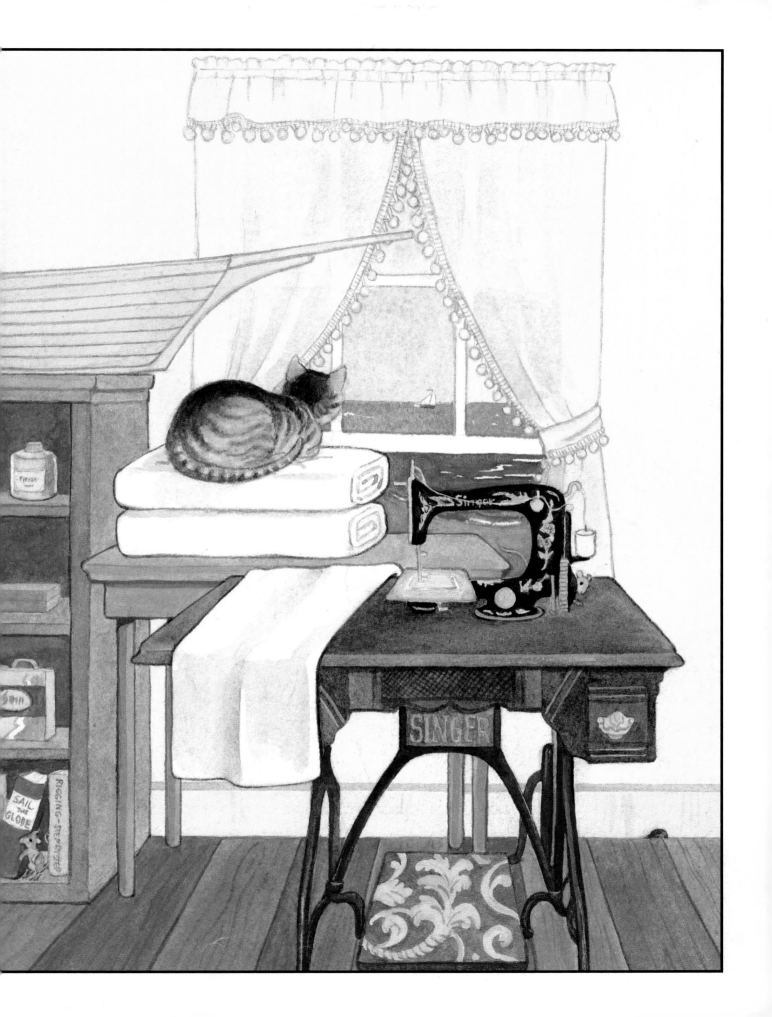

It was a small ship, but it was big enough to hold every last mouse.

Miss Renée printed up tiny tickets and passed them out.

"Where are we going?" asked the mice.

"Around the world," said Miss Renée, giving the boat a shove. "GOOD-BYE!"

Miss Renée began sweeping up after the mice.

At last, her big house and all her little houses were tidy and quiet again!

Maybe too quiet.

Without the mice, Miss Renée had trouble falling asleep at night. Much to her surprise, she missed their squeaky singing and pittery-pattery dancing. She missed the happy party sounds.

Each morning she went back to work making pine furniture and calico curtains and other beautiful things. But they didn't seem so beautiful anymore.

It was sad to think that no one would be sleeping in her little beds or switching on the electric lights and reading the miniature books. No one would serve tea in her teapots

or admire her vases of tiny tulips. No one would roll up her little braided rugs and dance a jig.

Miss Renée felt glum. She let out a long sigh.

Then she busied herself with her work and tried not to think about the mice.

Weeks passed, and then months. By the time whole seasons had passed, bringing autumn leaves and snowflakes and wildflowers, Miss Renée had almost forgotten about the mice.

…Until one day, when she looked out the window and saw a ship. At first she thought it was a big ship, far away.

But it was a small ship, very close.

She ran down to the ocean to meet it. "Where have you been?" she cried.

"Around the world, of course," said the mice, as they began unloading their cargo.

They had brought back rosewood from Bolivia and tulipwood from Burma. They had also brought mahogany from Honduras, hornbeam from Iran, and bamboo from China. There was silky-oak from Australia, koa wood from Hawaii, teak from Cameroon, and zebrawood from Zimbabwe.

The mice had brought fabric, too: tweed from England, tartan from Scotland, and lace and linen from Ireland. There was brocade from Belgium, velvet and satin from France, batik from Java, kente cloth from Ghana, madras from India, and brilliant woven cotton from Guatemala.

As if that weren't enough, they had also brought rice paper from Japan and marble from Italy and yak's wool from Tibet. And last but not least, a box of Turkish taffy and an enormous chocolate bar from Switzerland.

Miss Renée looked at the mice. She looked at all the beautiful things they had brought her from all over the world.

"Welcome home, mice!" she said.

No endangered trees were cut down by the mice in
this story. All wood was obtained from naturally fallen
branches, which were cut and milled with the kind
assistance of native mice and other small animals.
Also, the mice asked the Tibetan yak very politely for
some wool and gave her a basket of peaches in return.

Story © 2001 by Elizabeth Stokes Hoffman
Illustrations © 2001 by Dawn Peterson
ISBN 0-89272-505-2
Library of Congress Catalog Card Number: 00-111618
Printed in China

2 4 5 3 1

Down East Books
P.O. Box 679, Camden, ME 04843
Book orders: (800) 766-1670
www.downeastbooks.com

J.P. et
Hoffman

DATE DUE
